The Urbana Free Library

To renew: call **217-367-4057**
or go to **urbanafreelibrary.org**
and select **My Account**

"Bye, Mom and Dad," called Chris. "We're off to the mall to try and win a prize."

"Before you go, can you find a place for the manger scene?" his mom asked.

Chris frowned. "Why now? I did everything else. There's not much room left. After all, isn't the manger scene just another decoration?"

"Let's go!" exclaimed his friend Joy.

"See you, Mom," and out the door went Chris, Joy, and their robot, Gizmo.

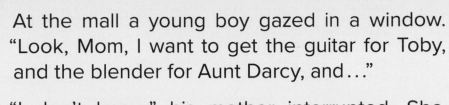

At the mall a young boy gazed in a window. "Look, Mom, I want to get the guitar for Toby, and the blender for Aunt Darcy, and..."

"I don't know," his mother interrupted. She looked so sad.

Chris watched it all; then the three friends went inside the mall just as a man was drawing a ticket for a big prize.

Just as the winner of the Christmas prize was about to be chosen, Gizmo yelled, "Watch out, Chris and Joy! Superbook is taking us somewhere."

"I'm taking you to see the most important gift the world has ever received," Superbook told them.

"Whee!" shouted Joy.

And in a wink of the eye the three friends landed in...somewhere.

"Where are we?" asked Joy.

"I have no idea. Whoa! What's that big shiny thing?" Chris's eyes became wider and wider as he realized what he was seeing. An angel!

"Shh!" Joy held her finger to her mouth. "Listen!"

"Do not be afraid, Mary, for you have found favor with God," the angel said. "Listen, you will bear a Son and shall call His name JESUS. He will be great and will be called the Son of the Highest. And of His kingdom there will be no end." Then Mary said to the angel, "How can this be, since I do not know a man?" The angel assured Mary, "With God nothing will be impossible."

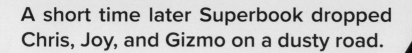

"Hello," Chris said to a man leading a donkey that carried a lovely young woman. Why, it was the same young woman who had talked with the angel!

"Can we walk along with you?"

"Yes, come along."

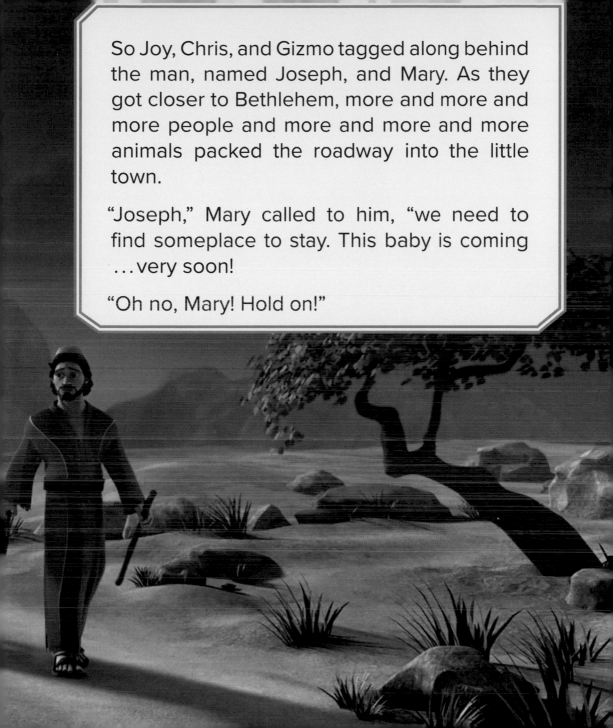

So Joy, Chris, and Gizmo tagged along behind the man, named Joseph, and Mary. As they got closer to Bethlehem, more and more and more people and more and more and more animals packed the roadway into the little town.

"Joseph," Mary called to him, "we need to find someplace to stay. This baby is coming …very soon!

"Oh no, Mary! Hold on!"

As soon as they got to the town of Bethlehem, Joseph began pounding on doors. "Can we stay here? Mary is going to have a baby…now!"

"No room here."

"No room here."

"No room here."

And then…finally… "Oh. There's a stable out back. Perhaps you can make her comfortable there."

Joseph wasted no time. Soon he had Mary as comfortable as he could make her on a bed of hay.

"Get the blankets from the donkey," Joseph told Chris, Joy, and Gizmo. "Then go get some clean water."

First they got the blankets, and then they went in search of water. Minutes later Jesus was born. Joseph looked at Mary as she wrapped the baby and laid Jesus in the manger.

Before Joy, Chris, and Gizmo found water, they found shepherds in fields near Bethlehem. The shepherds were taking care of a big flock of sheep—watching over them, making sure none of them fell down a hole, wandered off, or became some wild animal's dinner.

And you know what? Some of the shepherds were as young as you are. It was the kids' job to watch the sheep.

Sleepy shepherds—sleepy, sleepy eyes…just waiting and watching…and waiting…and watching—when all of a sudden…

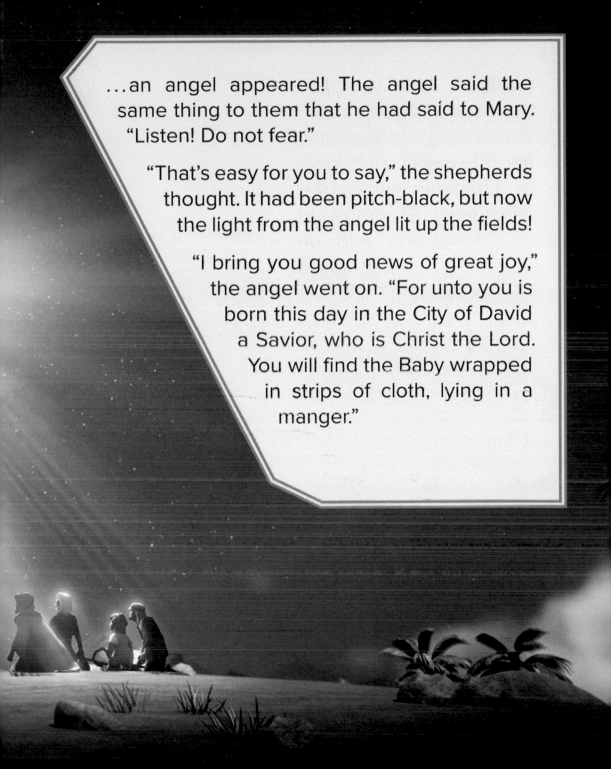

…an angel appeared! The angel said the same thing to them that he had said to Mary. "Listen! Do not fear."

"That's easy for you to say," the shepherds thought. It had been pitch-black, but now the light from the angel lit up the fields!

"I bring you good news of great joy," the angel went on. "For unto you is born this day in the City of David a Savior, who is Christ the Lord. You will find the Baby wrapped in strips of cloth, lying in a manger."

Suddenly the sky was filled with hundreds and hundreds and thousands and thousands of angels, all singing praise to God and saying, "Glory to God in the highest, and on earth peace, and good will toward men."

Standing nearby, Chris turned to look and said, "Did *you* see what *I* saw?"

"I did," said Joy.

"Did *you* hear what *I* heard?"

"I did!" said Gizmo.

"Well, why are we standing here?" Chris said. "Let's go to Mary and Joseph!"

So they started off with all the shepherds.

That little group of shepherds got to be the very first people in Bethlehem to see the baby. It was the most exciting moment of their lives! Why, it was the most exciting event ever to have happened on earth!

The shepherds were so happy about God's Son in the manger that they told everyone they met. Even wise men from far away came and brought amazing treasures as gifts for the baby.

In less time than it takes to say "Merry Christmas," Superbook whooshed the three travelers back to the mall.

Chris looked down at the prize ticket in his hand as the winning number was read aloud. "23463!"

"I won! I won!" he shouted. Then he stopped and saw the young boy who had been looking at presents in the mall window. For Christmas the boy only wanted to give gifts to others. Quietly Chris slid over to the boy and handed him the winning ticket. That little boy looked up with tears of happiness in his eyes.

"I just learned that giving is what Christmas is all about," Chris said to Joy and Gizmo. "God gave us the most important gift of all time—His Son, Jesus. It makes me want to give too."

As soon as Chris handed the winning ticket to the boy, the kids and Gizmo went home. Chris's mom had put the nativity on a table in the main hallway. Carefully Chris placed the baby Jesus in the manger.

"Do you know what I realized?" Chris said to his mom. "I realized that Christmas isn't about decorations and presents. It's about God giving us His Son, Jesus."

"And I learned that when God gave us His Son, Jesus, He gave the best that heaven had," chimed in Joy.

"Merry Christmas!" said Gizmo.